STARTING LINE READERS

Gymnastics JUMP

BY CC JOVEN

ART BY ED SHEMS

STONE ARCH BOOKS
a capstone imprint

Sports Illustrated Kids Starting Line Readers
is published by Stone Arch Books, a Capstone imprint
1710 Roe Crest Drive
North Mankato, Minnesota 56003
www.mycapstone.com

Sports Illustrated Kids is a trademark of Time Inc.
Used with permission.

Library of Congress Cataloging-in-Publication data
is available on the Library of Congress website.

ISBN: 978-1-4965-4250-2 (library binding)
ISBN: 978-1-4965-4257-1 (paperback)
ISBN: 978-1-4965-4261-8 (eBook pdf)

Summary: It's Lily's first gymnastics meet, and she is nervous.
Will she be able to complete all of her events without falling?

Printed in the United States of America
010056S17

This is Lily.

Lily likes gymnastics.

Today is her first meet.

Lily is excited.

Lily is nervous, too.

Lily stretches.

Lily does the splits.

Lily does a cartwheel.

Lily stretches more.

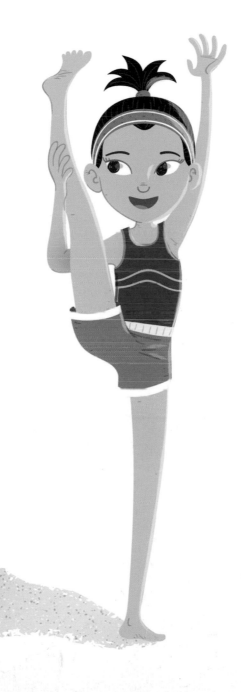

Lily is ready.

So is her team.

Lily does a handstand.

She does not fall.

Lily swings.

She does not fall.

Lily flips.

She does not fall.

Lily jumps.

Oh, no! Lily falls.

Lily feels sad.

But Lily gets back
on the beam.

Lily jumps.

She does not fall!

Lily feels happy.
So does her team.

Lily really likes gymnastics.

GYMNASTICS
WORD LIST

beam

cartwheel

flips

gymnastics

handstand

meet

stretches

swings

word
count: 91